Samuel French Acting Edition

The Wolves

by Sarah DeLappe

SAMUELFRENCH.COM   SAMUELFRENCH.CO.UK

MUSIC USE NOTE

Licensees are solely responsible for obtaining formal written permission from copyright owners to use copyrighted music in the performance of this play and are strongly cautioned to do so. If no such permission is obtained by the licensee, then the licensee must use only original music that the licensee owns and controls. Licensees are solely responsible and liable for all music clearances and shall indemnify the copyright owners of the play(s) and their licensing agent, Samuel French, against any costs, expenses, losses and liabilities arising from the use of music by licensees. Please contact the appropriate music licensing authority in your territory for the rights to any incidental music.

IMPORTANT BILLING AND CREDIT REQUIREMENTS

If you have obtained performance rights to this title, please refer to your licensing agreement for important billing and credit requirements.

THE WOLVES was produced by The Playwrights Realm (Katherine Kovner, Artistic Director; Roberta Pereira, Producing Director), at The Duke on 42nd St. in New York City on September 8, 2016. The performance was directed by Lila Neugebauer, with sets by Laura Jellinek, costumes by Asta Hostetter, lights by Lap Chi Chu, sound by Stowe Nelson, and wigs by Anne Ford-Coates. The Production Stage Manager was Lori Lundquist. The cast was as follows:

#11	Susannah Perkins
#25	Lauren Patten
#13	Jenna Dioguardi
#46	Tedra Millan
#2	Sarah Mezzanotte
#7	Brenna Coates
#14	Samia Finnerty
#8	Midori Francis
#00	Lizzy Jutila
SOCCER MOM	Mia Barron

THE WOLVES was remounted on December 5, 2016 by special arrangement with Scott Rudin and Eli Bush. The producers, location, director, and design team remained the same. The Production Stage Manager was Amanda Spooner. The cast remained the same, except:

SOCCER MOM	Kate Arrington

Originally presented by New York Stage and Film and Vassar in the Powerhouse Season, Summer 2016.

Playwrights Horizons Theater School produced a workshop of *The Wolves* in 2015 in association with Clubbed Thumb, where the play had been developed previously.

Winner of the 2016 Sky Cooper New American Play Prize at Marin Theatre Company, Mill Valley, California (Jasson Minadakis, Artistic Director; Keri Kellerman, Managing Director).

Produced by Lincoln Center Theater, New York City, 2017.

CHARACTERS

#11 – Midfield. Brainy, morbid, budding elitist, thoughtful. Seventeen.

#25 – Defense. Captain. Classic (ex.)coach's daughter. Seventeen.

#13 – Midfield. Stoner, older pot dealer brother, into her wackiness. Sixteen.

#46 – Bench. New girl. Awkward, different, just wants to fit in. Sixteen.

#2 – Defense. Innocent, unlucky, kind, skinny. Sixteen.

#7 – Striker. Too cool for school. Sarcastic, "fuck," thick eyeliner. Almost seventeen.

#14 – Midfield. #7's insecure sidekick. Just switched to contacts. Sixteen.

#8 – Defense. Childlike and determined to stay that way. Sixteen.

#00 – Goalie. Intense performance anxiety, perfectionist, high achiever. Seventeen.

SOCCER MOM

SETTING

An indoor soccer field somewhere in suburban America. The field is AstroTurf. We only see the field: no goals, no bleachers. Fans, fluorescents. There should be the sense that the field goes on forever.

Winter. Saturdays.

SPEED

The play should take ninety minutes.

AUTHOR'S NOTES

Each scene is a warm-up for a game. The warm-up is a series of exactly-timed stretches: lunges, quads, hamstrings, butterfly, etc. The team executes it wordlessly, in perfect unison and with military precision.

Over the course of the play, #46 learns the warm-up.

In Week Three, if #46 can't juggle a soccer ball, she should perform footwork or tricks to the rhythm of the yogurt chant. It ought to be an impressive show of ball-handling skill.

In Time-Out, #00 must exhaust herself with great feats of athleticism and strength that build to the final scream. What that sequence looks like is open to interpretation. It could be kicking soccer balls offstage. In our production, the actor devised an escalating series of exercises, including high knees, butt kicks, burpees, jumping jacks, etc.

In the passing drill in Week Three, p. 56-63, the team pairs off into duos or trios as illustrated by the discrete columns of text. Characters should only be onstage when they have text in their column. They should enter passing the soccer ball when their column begins until they pass it off as their column terminates. The idea is that we're catching the snippets of conversation that transpire while each pair moves through this particular patch of turf. The stage should never be empty and there should be no dead air between the transitions from one pair to another.

PUNCTUATION NOTE

(text in parentheses) – sotto voce

(bold text in parentheses) – orange slice in mouth

We are always the same age inside.

Gertrude Stein

WEEK ONE – THE CAMBODIAN

nine girls in uniform stretch in a circle on an AstroTurf indoor soccer field
they do the same stretch at the same time for the same amount of time

#11.

    but it's like
    he's old

#25.

    he murdered 1000s of people

#13.

    literally 100s of 1000s

             #2.

             (to #8, quiet)
             have you played with it before?

#11.

    yeah but did you see the photo?

             #8.

             what?

#46.

    what photo

#13.

    the photo

             #2.

             nothing

#25.

    oh yeah the photo

             #14.*

             what'd you say?

             #2.

             (a little louder)
             have you played with it before

             #7.

             like yeah of course we have
             We're Women
             that's like what we do

#11.

    yeah he's like 90 years old

---

* **#14** has a cold this week

#11.

and like has the old person eyes

> **#2.**
>
> has it been a problem?

#11.

and all these wrinkles
and like gave testimony on Skype from his hospital bed

> **#7.**
>
> like has blood run down my legs?

> **#14** *laughs hysterically*

#25.

I don't think they have Skype in Cambodia

#13.

that is like so

#25.

what

#13.

like so bad

> **#8.**
>
> it's really no big deal

#13.

like you can't say that
cause it's like

#11.

yeah

#13.

insensitive

> **#8.**
>
> seriously

#25.

no
no it's not
it's not insensitive

#11.

they definitely have Skype in Cambodia

#25.

the internet isn't the internet everywhere you guys

#46.

are you talking about Cambodia?

> **#2.**
>
> *(terrified)*
> what if like my pad falls out?

#13.

that's the stupidest shit

#11.

no
she's right

        #8.

        omigosh

#25.

yeah
(thank you)
it's like
like here we can look up whatever we want

        #7.

        you still use those?

#25.

but like in China they don't have Twitter in China

        #7.

        that's like running around with a diaper or something

        #14.

        you gotta get off of those

#11.

well that's not exactly

        #14.

        you want a ?
        cause I can get you one

        #8.

        same

      #2 *shakes head no*

        #7.

        no you want it
        trust me you want it

#11.

I'm pretty sure they have a Twitter like platform in China

        #14.

        (motions off)
        they're just in my backpack

        #2.

        (on the verge of tears)
        no
        thank you

#25.

uh platform?

#8.
   you should like totally take one

#2.
   yeah

#13.
   are you saying
   you're on Chinese Twitter
   or something?

#11.
   no

#11.
   I'm not on Chinese

#11.
   I'm just

#11.
   I mean like
   yeah we *should*
   take our liberties for granted

#13.
   um

#11.
   what

#13.
   um no we should not

           #7.
              wait

#13.
   we should like definitely not
   take our liberties for granted

           #7.
              what if it ran down and like

#11.
   I never said we should take our liberties for granted

           #7.
              stained the ball

#13.
   um

#25.
   you did

#8.
it's not so hard
you just like
pop!
I have like
special sporty ones
like the ones on tv

#2.
we don't have a tv

#8.
omigosh
that's so sad!
I always forget that
about you

#7.
   (you remember Courtney)

#14.
   (oh jesus Courtney)

#7.
   (with the super plus)

#14.
   (oh my god yes)

#7.
   little perv

#14.
   hahaha
   hahaha
   hahaha

#2.

what?

#8.

ew

#11.

no
I didn't

#14.

that would be like so epic

#11.

I would never say that

#14.

like so scary for the other team

#46.

I've been to Cambodia

#7.

yeah like
"score on me with my own baby blood?
I think not!"

#13.

we should be like very very thankful for our liberties you know

#14.

yeah ha like

#11.

oh my god I like totally know and believe in that
guys you know what I

#46.

(louder)
I've been to Phnom Penh

#14.

"want a piece of me?
here! have a piece of my / ovary"

#11.

/ I am like

#7.

yeah like

pause to think of joke

#11.

firmly pro-liberty

#14.

totally

#14.
haha

#7.
like you know
uh

#11.
I just meant / like

#7.
/ suck my tampon bitchesssss!

#14.
hahaha yeahhh

#13.
DUDE!

#25.
hey

#8.
gross!

#14.
"you got my period on your cleats fool"

#13.
haha nasty

#7.
SUCK IT

#25.
HEY

#8.
you guys are being soooo gross

*#2 abruptly stands up
jogs away from the circle*

#8.
yay! she's doing it!
you go girl!

#2.
no I just um
I have to go to the portaparty
…portapotty

#13.
portaparty?
more like
portapartaaay

#14.
take one
seriously
they're in my backpack in a little polka dot thing

#7.
RUN BITCH RUN

#25.
language

#7 and #14 exchange an eye-roll

#8.
(to #7)
you know she doesn't like that word

#25.
HUSTLE BACK
KICK-OFF'S IN TEN

#7.
I don't like your face
doesn't mean it doesn't exist

#14.

GUYSGUYSGUYS:
she uses pads

#11.

really?

#7.

yep

#13.

weird

#8.

(scolding)
you guys her family is like super religious

#11.

um what does that have to do with her feminine product of choice

#13.

word up

#8.

I just don't think we should call her
we shouldn't use the
the b-word

#7.

bitch

#14.

ha biotch

#25.

hey

#14.

oh my god it is just like a female dog!

#13.

I hear she like
she like speaks in tongues

#8.

 no she doesn't

#13.

 that's not what Kristen told me

#8.

she doesn't
she goes to my stepmom's church
she's Episcopalian

#13.

(speaking in tongues aka ululation)
lalalalalala

#11.

I saw this documentary on Netflix
about like snake handling
have you guys heard about snake handling

#7.

more like
Bitch-co-palian

#13.

(tongues become more of a song)
lalalalalala

#11.

all these southerners like die of snakebites
while like communing with god
it's so dark

#25.

why would you watch a documentary?

#11.

I dunno
it's cool stuff

#14.

or like
like
E-bitch-co-palian

#7.

um hello
just made that joke

#14.

ha yeah you did

#7.

shut up whore

#14.

ha ha shut it you uh
you uh

#7.

make me bitch

#14.

...ok

> **#14** *slaps* **#7** *in boob*

#11.

they have so many options on there
you should check it out

#25.

but for fun?
you do that for fun?

#11.

yeah
or like
on family movie night
(to #13)
would you shut up?

#25.

you guys do movie nights?

#11.

I don't want to talk about it

#13.

lalalalalala
lalalalalala
lalalalalala
lalalalalala
lalalalalala
lalalalalala
lalalalalala
lalalalalala
lalalalalala
lalalala

did you say
family
mooooovie
night?

#7.

OW!

#25.

Ladies

#14.

(to #7)
baby

#7.

that hurt asshole

#14.

faker baby

#7.

fuck you they're really tender right now

#25.

Ladies

#46.

(trying to get in on the fun)
is it because you are pregnant?

long awkward pause

#8.

were you guys talking about the Khmer Rouge?

#11.

yeah

#8.

did you read that

#11.

that article yeah

#46.

what article

#8.

so horrible

#11.

yeah

#46.

guys what article

#7.

(to #46)
would you shut the fuck up?

#13.

    I thought it was *(mispronounces Khmer Rouge)*

#11.

    no I'm pretty sure it's Khmer Rouge

#13.

    oh Khmer Rouge

#8.

    yeah Khmer Rouge

#13.

    (British accent)
    Khmer Rouge

#11.

    you are such an idiot

#13.

    whatever
    I read it and like couldn't tell

#14.

    what's the Khmer Rouge

#13.

    they're like Nazis in Cambodia

#25.

    but in the 70s

#11.

    that's not / quite

#7.

    / you don't know about the Khmer Rouge?

#14.

    no
    am I supposed to?
    am I supposed to know about the Khmer Rouge?

        #00 *stands up and looks sick and jogs off*

#11.

    they don't teach you about Cambodia at St. Albert?

#14.

    um I don't think so

#11.

    (superior)
    Oh

#7.

    we don't do genocides 'til senior year

#14.

    (to #7)
    (hey)
    (hey)
    (hey)

#7.

    (what)

#14.

    (are you ok?)

        #7 *rolls her eyes*

#8.

I am getting such a bad grade in social studies
that Armenia project killed me

#14.

(to #7)

how do you know about the Khmer Rouge

#7.

I don't know
it's the Khmer Rouge

#46.

like Hermione right
when I was little I thought it was like "Herm-ee-oh / n"

#14.

/ were we talking about fucking Harry Potter?
um no we were talking about the Khmer Rouge
the Khmer Rouge ok
who were like Asian Nazis
and killed billions of people
so like have a sense of like of like

#7.

not being a dick about it

> **#2** *jogs back on and rejoins stretch circle*

#11.

it was 100s of 1000s of people
not billions

#8.

(did you try it?)

#14.

whatever

> **#2** *vigorously shakes no*

#8.

(omigosh you should
you should take one
or at least try it)

#11.

that makes a huge difference
there are only like 7 billion people on the entire planet

> **#2** *awkwardly smiles*

#14.

 ok

#8.

(they're supes comfortable)

#11.

it's just factually inaccurate

#14.

yeah I get it I was just like making a point

> **#2** *awkwardly smiles*

#11.

but it wasn't the right point

#8.

pop!

#13.

cha-ching

#14.

does it matter?
does it really

#11.

yeah
I think it does
I mean of course it does

#25.

you're the one who said you felt bad cause he was old

#13.

yeah
you were like "oh they can't execute him he's 90"
when he killed 100s of 1000s of human beings

#7.

but he killed all those people

#11.

no that's not what I /

#2.

what's she talking about?

#13.

she like pities the Cambodian dude just cause he's stupid old

#2.

the who?

#13.

you know the guy
uh
like uh
new-a
noo-o

#11.

I thought it was chee
or like chi
or something

#13.

no I think it was like
with an n
pretty sure it was
with an n

#2.

(to #11)
you feel bad for him?

#11.

no I don't feel bad I just

#25.

have you done social studies?

#2.

the article response?

#25.

yeah

#2.

oh

#25.

yeah

#2.

he enslaved and exterminated his own people

#8.

yeah wow

#11.

no guys I just think it's uh
it's
(finding the word) ethically complicated

#13.

what's so complicated about killing 100s of 1000s of people?

#7.

well it's probably pretty challenging
technically

#14.	**#11.**	**#13.**		**#8.**	
wow	um	that is gnarly man		eww	**#2** *shakes head*

#7.

what
think about it

     #25 *sighs*

#11.

no what I meant was like
ok I do think it was horrible
obviously
he was horrible

     #00 *jogs back on and rejoins the circle*

#13.

IS horrible

#11.

yeah ok IS horrible
but
I think it's interesting

#2.

it's not interesting
it's like evil

#11.

ok but
imagine if you did something horrible today
but you didn't think it was horrible

#2.

but it was horrible
is the thing
it was /

#11.

let me finish
it was horrible
it was an an atrocity
right?

#13.

yeah
it was

#11.

but YOU didn't think it was an atrocity
you thought you were like saving your country
like destroying the enemy to save your own people

#2.

but the enemy WAS your own people

#25.

yeah

#11.

right
I know that
but like
what if
after you did that
you just like lived your life
like went to college and got a job and got married and had kids and grandkids and

#13.

whoa

#11.

and then
when you were 90 and like on the verge of death with like uh emphysema
that's when an INTERPOL guy knocks on your door and is like
we found you
we know what you did
and guess what?
you're going to prison
For Life

    long pause as it sinks in

#46.

my grandma has emphysema

    no one really notices that comment

#8.

prison for life?
he's only going to prison for life?

#11.

yeah

#8.

but he's 90

he's probably going to die soon

#11.

Pol Pot's already dead

most of 'em the big ones already dead

#13.

freaky deeky

#2.

didn't he Skype into court from his hospital bed

#11.

yeah that's right

he's super sick

#2.

so he might only serve a year in prison

for doing a genocide?

#11.

yeah

#7.

that is so fucked

whistle blows
everyone looks off

#25.

alright

let's go let's go

the girls start to stand and get ready

#8.

who are we playing again?

#25.

the Hornets

#8.

right

#13.

those guys blow

#11.

remember Las Vegas Showcase last year?

#00 smiles

#7.

this girl remembers

#00 *blushes*

#7.

you were like
"shoot on my goal?
I think not"

#14.

ha ha

#11.

7-0 baby

#25.

4th in our bracket

#8.

and then we went to Circus Circus!
guys remember Circus Circus?
with the elephants?

#2.

there were elephants?

#11.

yeah

#8.

yeah
in the big tent

#13.

look at their stupid yellow jerseys
they look like like like
school buses

#2.

…I don't remember any elephants

#7.

yeah
fucking school buses

#14.

school buses

#13.

schoooool busssesssss

they laugh

#25.

come on
let's get on out there
Coach is waiting

general eye-roll

#14.

Coach couldn't give a shit if we paid him

#7.

oh that's right
we do

#11.

he's like so hungover

it's embarrassing

#2.

he is?

#11.

why do you think he wears those stupid athletic sunglasses
Inside
on a Saturday Morning?

#7.

maybe he's still wasted

#14.

definitely

#25.

(ignoring that)
hustle girls

#2.

maybe he's just sleepy

#13.

oh bleedy
sweet sweet little bleedy

#11.

he's definitely still wasted

#7.

such a joke

> **#14** *has a coughing attack*
> *everyone looks at her*

#25.

are you sick?

#14.

no

#25.

you sound a little

#11.

yeah

#13.

yeah you sound all like *(nasal sounds)*

#14.

(sniffling)
I feel so good you guys

#25.

I don't want you here if you're sick

#14.

I am totally fine

#14.

> it's just like
> allergies

#25.   **#13.**

> ...alright   right right
> get on out there   turf allergies
> hustle

                                                             #8.

#7.

                                                             is that a thing?

> you better not get me sick before my birthday

#14.

> um I am so not sick

> > **#14** *and* **#7** *jog off*

#13.

> *(to #2)*
> btdubs I think we've synced

#2.

> excuse me?

#13.

> I mean
> we've like
> our bodies bleed together

#8.

> ewwww

#11.

> gross

#13.

> you bleed I bleed
> catch my drift

#2.

> *(horrified and small)*
> cool

#11.

> that happened to me and my sister
> our bathroom is ugh
> it's like a mass grave in that trash can

> > **#13, #2, #11, #8** *run off*
> > **#25** *goes up to* **#46,** *who is struggling to tie her shoes*

#25.

> um hey

#46.

> hello

#25.

> can we talk for a sec?

#46.

    yes I have lots of secs

        slight pause
        neither wants to acknowledge what she just said

#25.

    it's just uh
    ok uh
    try not to make jokes like that

#46.

    what joke?

#25.

    the uh
    the you know

        #46 *gives a blank look*

#25.

    the uh pregnancy?
    …joke?

#46.

    oh

#25.

    (nods)
    yeah
    yeah

#46.

    why?

#25.

    what?

#46.

    why can't I make a pregnancy joke?

        pause

#25.

    I mean
    we like to have fun but
    you know
    uh
    "if you can't say something nice
    don't say anything at all"?

        pause

#25.

    (captain mode)
    great
    let's get on out there

#46.

   could I play striker?

#25.

   7 is striker

   …7 has always been striker

#46.

   oh

#25.

   it's just

   we're undefeated

   and we want to stay undefeated

   right?

   especially with the college showcase tournament coming up?

#46.

   …it's the only spot in football I haven't tried yet

   I just thought

   it might be easier

         football??

#25.

   …it never gets easier

   you just get better

   …

   that's something my dad

   …

   (energetic) I'll sub you in ASAP

   kay?

   now let's get out there and kick some Hornet boo-tay!

         #25 *jogs off*
         #00 *is still wrapping her hands*
         #46 *drinks her water bottle and lets it hang from her mouth, lost in thought*

#00.

   she had an abortion

#46.

   what?

         #00 *doesn't look up from her hands*

#46.

   when?

#00.

   two months ago

         #00 *puts on her goalie gloves*

#00.

   just cause Nuon Chea's weak

   doesn't mean he shouldn't pay

#46 *doesn't know how to respond to this*

#00.

the Cambodian?
he deserves it
even if he's weak
he deserves it

  whistle

WEEK TWO – TODOS LOS NIÑOS

eight girls in uniform stretch in a circle on an AstroTurf indoor soccer field
they do the same stretch at the same time for the same amount of time

#2.

I'm talking about Mexican children in cages

#11.

not just Mexican
mostly like Guatemalan and Honduran and like   **#2.**
all over   in cages!
all over Central America   cages!

#7.*

and that's why you're selling scarves?

#2.

I'm knitting them myself
well with Amnesty International
the whole club's knitting them
or I guess learning how to knit

#13.

and they cost how much?

#2.

25 dollars

#25.

jeez

#2.

I know but it's for a good cause

#8.

I always want to call it Middle America

#14.

what?

#8.

Central America
I always want to call it Middle America
does anyone else do that?
Middle America?

#13.

like Middle Earth?

#8.

omigosh

---

* #7 has a cold this week

#11.

    uh it's Meso America
    technically

                                 #2.

                                     I have some in my backpack
                                     if anyone wants to

#8.

    Middle Earth!
    omigoshhhhh

                                   #2.

#11.

    and uh we are Middle America
    I mean we live in Middle America   you can choose the yarn color

#14.

    what does that mean

#11.

    it means we're like   #7.
    we're America   USA
    you know   USA

#13.   #7 & #14.

    right totally like   USA
    we're not High America   USA
    we're not Low America
    we're just like America America

#11.

    it's like
    you know
    we drive pick-up trucks and don't like cuss words   #7.

                                      the fuck is a cuss word

#8.

    (sigh)   #14.
    I'd love a pick-up truck   ha   #25.

                                                               Hey

#13.

    (to #11)
    doesn't your mom drive a Prius?

#8.

    like a big purple pick-up truck

#11.

    yeah but
    you know

#13.

    how is Dr. Feinstein doing these days?

#11.

    (wary)
    she's uh
    she's great

#13.

still got that smoking haircut?
and that sexy sexy bod?

#11.

screw you

#13.   **#7.**

you have got a Hot Mom   um I think you meant "fuck"
those are the cards you were dealt
and you know what   **#25.**
you gotta make a certain kind of peace with that   cut it out

#11.

she is not a Hot Mom!

#13.

(to #11)
that's not what Kevin says
as he jerks off to her website pic

#11.   **#8.**

that's so wrong   ewwww
he's her patient

#14.

Kevin sees a shrink?

#13.

uh Kevin?
hello?
Kevin?
the community college drop-out who sells pot from our basement?
he's like why shrinks were invented

#11.

She's
My
Mom

#13.

and He's My Brother!
that makes us like
oh man
if my brother's banging your mom
that makes me your

#11.

you are such an asshole

#13.

that's Auntie Asshole to you dearie

#7.   **#25.**

that is so nasty   Ladies

#8.

GUYS!
omigosh you guys
does that mean we're hobbits?

#13.

um
whaaaaat

#8.

cause like we live in
Middle America
so like Middle Earth
so like... The Shire

#2.

you are beyond obsessed

#8.

I love that
I like love that we live in The Shire of America

#11.

that is not what Middle America

#13.

try telling that to the future Mrs. Samwise Gamgee

#8.

(dreamy)
he's just such a good friend!
you know?

#7.

ACHOO

#14.

bless you

#7.

thanks bitch

#7.

jesus

        #13 sings the Shire theme from The Lord of the Rings, with **#8** and then **#2** joining in*

#7.

you guys are retarded

#8.

hey
don't use the r-word

#2.

yeah
not cool

#7.

oh get over yourselves

---

* A license to produce **THE WOLVES** does not include a performance license for any songs from **THE LORD OF THE RINGS**. The publisher and author suggest that the licensee contact ASCAP or BMI to ascertain the music publisher and contact such music publisher to license or acquire permission for performance of the song. If a license or permission is unattainable for **THE SHIRE THEME SONG** the licensee may not use the song in **THE WOLVES** but may create an original meoldy in the same style. For further information, please see Music Use Note on page 2.

#25.

> no really
> it's really not cool

#7.

> jesus you guys are like a bunch of fascists
> haven't you heard of like free speech
> like the first fucking amendment?

#25.

> it's just an ugly word
> and it's not the sort of word we want on the field

#7.

> (fuck you)

#25.

> what was that?

#7.

> nothing

#25.

> what?

#7.

> jesus nothing

> *pause*

#11.

> hey where's the new girl?

> *pause*

#14.

> I suppose we'll just have to like manage without her

> *titters*

#25.

> girls

> *slight pause*

#8.

> who are we playing again?

#25.

> Fusion

> *they all look off to the other team warming up*

#13.

> are they any good?

#25.

> they're ok
> great goalie

#14.

> oh right

The Wall

#11.

hey we've got a great goalie right here

#13.

ow ow ow

> *#13 grabs #00's shoulders and she grimaces*

#8.

she's so huge
just look at her

#7.

Christine Fucking Kratzer

#14.

you think she lifts?

#11.

she has to
to get that kind of muscle def

#2.

I should lift more

#13.

um what?
why?

#2.

nobody sees me on the field and is like "uh-oh"

#13.

you could like get a facial tattoo
like a full-on facial tattoo

#14.

yeah but you're so skinny

#2.

no I'm not

#8.

omigosh you so totally are

#11.

yeah

#2.

no I'm not I'm really not you guys

#25.

if you want to bulk up maybe you should try lifting

#7.

and like eating more protein

#2.

I eat plenty of protein
I like basically live on peanut butter and cheese!
(deeply frustrated) ECH

#8.

hey it's ok
I don't have any upper body strength either

#2.

I just can't stop thinking about it

#8.

really?

#2.

all those Mexican kids in cages!

#11.

they're not just / Mexican

#2.

there's so many of them
and they're all stuck in these camps

#8.

ohhh
hahaha
omigosh
I thought you were
talking about biceps!
hahaha

#13.

that sounds ok

#2.

no like not fun campsreally horrible camps
and some of them are like Travis's age!

#8.

that's super sad
I like didn't know about this at all

#13.

los niños
todos los niños
ay mamacita los pobrecitos

#2.

I just really hope someone's reading to them
5 to 6 is a really important age
especially for ESL

#11.

you know you're being racist

#8.

I love reading to Patrick
it's sooo fun
I get to do all the voices
like "here comes grumpy Mr. Platypus"

#13.

que?

#11.

like super racist

#13.

lo siento
tia mia
pero no hablo tu lengua estupida

#2.

in my youth ministry we tutor 1st graders
at Jessie Beck
they're all ESL kids
and the later they come over the / harder it is

#11.

it's idioma? / actually?

#7.

ARE YOU GUYS FUCKING BRAIN DEAD?
these kids have Nowhere to go
no like Legal Status
I mean they're just going to be like Deported
back to their Families who Sent them here
so they could like Have a Better Life
and like not live in a fucking War Zone with like fucking Drug Lords
but now if they like If they even make it across the fucking Border
they're stuck
in like basically Prisons in like Arizona
and being used as like as like FUCKING POLITICAL PROPS!

#13.

…whoa man

#2.

…what are you saying

#7.

so they have much bigger fucking problems than
than fucking
than fucking ESL BEDTIME STORIES

#14.

I didn't know you cared about this stuff

#7.

my dad's firm
does like a lot of immigration stuff
pro bono stuff
he's so pissed

#2.

we're pissed too!
we're super pissed!
that's why we're knitting scarves!

#8.

but like
didn't it take you a while to learn English?

#7.

me?

#8.

(to #14)
no no you

#14.

…um what do / you

#8.

like cause your family came over when you were four?
didn't it take you a while?

#14.

    um no

    I already spoke English

#8.

    oh! ok

    I guess that's why you don't have a Mexican uh

#14.

    ...I'm Armenian

#8.

    oh!

    ...cool

    that's so cool

#13.

    dude!

#11.

    we just learned all about Armenia

#14.

    yeah

    I'm uh

    I'm Armenian

#8.

    then why are you always going to Mexico with your family?

#14.

    um for vacation?

#8.

    ohhhh

#11.

    seriously?

#2.

    her dad's Armenian

#14.

    yeah my dad's Armenian

    my mom's American

    they were living in London when they had me

#13.

    ay yay yay chica

#8.

    super cool

#11.

    do you have double citizenship?

    I want double citizenship

    ...dual

#25.

    that's so cool

#2.

    I knew that

#13.

    ello, guvnor!

    the loo! the lorry!

    the... LON-DON!

#8.

    wait shouldn't you have like an English accent then?

#7.

    YOU GUYS ARE RETARDED

#13.

whoa man

#25.

would you watch that language

#7.

oh yeah?
or WHAT?

#25.

or I'll tell Coach

#7.

oh no!
the dumbass who works at Best Buy?
see how many fucks I give

#25.

that's it
I'm warning you

#7.

fuck
you

#25.

you're running laps

#7.

I HATE YOU
I HATE YOU
I
HATE
YOU

> *#7 storms off*

#25.

well
we'll uh
we'll see if she starts this game huh

> *pause*

#13.

(shouldn't you uh)

#14.

…(yeah)
(yeah)

> *#14 jogs off after #7*
> *#46 walks in wearing a puffy coat over street clothes and odd snow boots*

#13.

there go our Lady Crusaders

#11.

St. Albert has like the most Catholic team name

#13.

could be like the Lady Jesus
the Lady Jesus's
the Lady Jesi?

#8.

guys I totally thought she was Mexican

#2.

I knew she was Armenian
her nana used to make these Armenian pastries

#8.

I forgot you guys used to be like best best friends

#2.

yeah
she taught me how to knit when I was like 7
we'd knit and watch Power Rangers in her den

#13.

GO GO POWER RANGERS!

#8.

guys I feel horrible
was that horrible?

#11.

(to #8)
it's not a bad thing
to be Mexican

#8.

no I know I just

#46.

I've been to Armenia

slight pause where they notice her

#25.

oh!
hey!
you made it!

#46.

sorry
my bus

#25.

...that's great!
get changed and get back out here
alright?

#13.

viva la Mexica!

#11.

it's viva Mexico

#13.

viva Mexico!

#11.

you are THE MOST annoying

#13.

(her bus?)

> #46 *just stands there*

#25.

what's up?

#46.

the locker room's closed

#25.

oh yeah uh
hm

#11.

portapotty?

> #46 *looks uncomfortable*

#25.

yeah I guess you should use the portapotty
sorry

> #46 *stands for a sec and then walks off*

#13.

she takes the bus?

#11.

she told me she has to take like 3 buses to get here

#8

wow

#13.

doesn't she live in like the hills?

#8

really?

#13.

yeah I heard she lives in the hills in this like yogurt thing with her mom

#2.

she lives in a yogurt?

> #46 *walks back on*
> *she forgot her backpack*

#46.

...backpack

> #46 *grabs it and walks off*

#13.

I can't imagine being homeschooled

#25.

yeah

#11.

totally

#8.

    yeah

    so weird

#13.

    she doesn't even have a school season

    you know

#8.

    and it's like so weird she just joined our team

#11.

    nobody does that

#8.

    I mean we've been playing together forever

#2.

    remember The Blossoms

#13.

    (to #25)

    oh man when your dad was our coach

#11.

    Coach Frank

#13.

    good ol' Screamy Screamy Coach Frank

#25.

    (embarrassed)

    yeah

    yeah

#11.

    can always tell when Frank's around

#13.

    first one in the lawn chair

    first one out of the lawn chair

    punching a ref in the face

#25.

    that was two years ago

#2.

    he just cares a lot

#8.

    but like

    she's only now playing indoor?

    like – really?

#25.

    I mean

    she's pretty good

    for having never played before

#13.

wait
whaaaaat

#2.

seriously?

#8.

she's never played before??
like ever?

#25.

that's what she said on her registration form

#8.

omigosh

#11.

you get to see the registration forms?

#13.

like on a team?
or like indoor?
or like at all?

#25.

I don't know

#11.

like all the registration forms?

#25.

yeah uh
Coach showed them to me

#8.

wow
then she's like a
wow she's like a prodigy

#13.

yeah dude

#25.

I asked her if she wanted to play travel team
and she was like
"what's travel team"

#13.

NO

#8.

omigosh

#11.

they just moved here you know

#25.

and she called it "football"

#11.

what??

#13.

like as a joke?

#25.

yeah she called soccer "football"
and positions "spots"

#13.

as a joke
right?

#8.

that is like so sad

#25.

I don't think so

#13.

truth to power?
she's pretty stinky

#8.

omigosh I know

#11.

she doesn't shave

#8.

like anywhere?

#13.

WHOA is she even like American?

#2.

guys should we really be

#13.

what

#2.

…like behind her back
I don't feel comfortable with uh
you know

　　　　pause

#13.

uh
ok

　　　　#00 *stands up and runs off looking sick*

#25.

hope they finish construction soon

#8.

yeah that portapotty is like so disgusting

#13.

> yeah last week
> after the game
> someone was in there for like EVER
> and I really had to go
> but like finally finally they open the door
> and it was
> you won't even believe it:
> Louise

#11.

> no

#13.

> yeah
> oh yeah
> Lou-ise

#25.

> Louise Peterson?

#13.

> yep
> yep

#8.

> what was she doing here?

#13.

> and of course I get in there and she took like the HUGEST dump

#8.

> ewwww

#11.

> did not need to know that

#25.

> I think she's sort of cool

#13.

> ...dude
> what??

#2.

> who's Louise Peterson?

#11.

> oh she's that new girl
> super punk

#8.

> she sang in that coffee house?
> and like licked the microphone?

#2.

> oh

#2.

her

#13.

you think she's sorta cool?

#8.

she is so WEIRD

#25.

I don't know

#8.

she smells like cigarettes

#13.

she has such a creepy laugh
she sits behind me in precalc
and does this weird little creepy laugh

#8.

and her hair
she has weird hair
it's like
pokey

#13.

"he he he"
"he he he"

#11.

ha ha

#25.

yeah

#13.

"he he he"

#25.

ok ok

> **#46** *walks on in uniform*

#25.

I just think she's sorta different

#13.

"oh Louise
you're just
sorta
different"

> **#13** *fake makes out with Louise*

#8.

ewww

#25.

    (blushing)
    guys that's
    you're being so immature
    she's really smart
    we're in the same AP English / class and

#46.

    (loudly, to #2)
    / I think you meant yurt

#2.

    (very polite)
    …excuse me?

#46.

    you said yogurt
    I think you meant yurt
    I live in a yurt with my mom

#2.

    …oh

#46.

    you can't really live in a yogurt

        uneasy laughter

#46.

    hey I uh just saw the uh

        can't remember her name

#46.

    uh goalie? outside? and I think she's /

#11.

    vomiting?

        #13 *makes the sound*

#8.

    ewwwww

        #13 *makes the sound on #8*

#8.

    stop stop stop

#46.

    (confused that they know this is happening)
    yeah uh
    is she alright?

#25.

    she vomits before every game

#13.

    and she stops talking
    like totally clams up

#11.

    it's a nervous condition

#8.

    it's like disgusting is what it is

#11.

    she's like super high functioning

#13.

    basically a genius

#25.

    she has a 4.9
    and edits The East Gazette

#11.

    I'm a columnist

#2.

    she has a 4.9?

#8.

    and plays the saxophone in State Youth Orchestra

#25.

    and leads Model UN

#11.

    but crippling SAD

#2.

    she's not very sad

#11.

    no no
    SAD
    S.A.D.
    Social Anxiety Disorder

#46.

    oh
    well that explains that I guess

        light laughter
        awkward silence

#46.

    I think there's a bird in the air dome

        they all look up

#25.

that happens sometimes

#11.

what I want to know is how they get in

#13.

dude I do not want to be in here
if there's a hole in the air dome

#11.

I think we'd be ok

#8.

there's a hole in the air dome?

#13.

nuh uh have you like SEEN a balloon pop before

#11.

um I think it's more complicated than that

awkward silence

#46.

…you can tell by the rusty flanks

awkward-er silence

#46.

(trying to gossip)
hey so uh who knows about the abortion?

pause

#13.

wow

pause

#25.

that's uh
we don't say stuff like that

#46.

(totally mortified)
cool

#13.

I thought she just took Plan B

#8.

that's not what I heard

#2.

where?

#46.

right there
on top of the ventilation unit

#2.

where?

#46.

(pointing) there

#2.

oh!
pretty

#46.

I think it's a tufted
titmouse

#13.

no I'm pretty sure it was just Plan B

#11.

maybe she had an abortion
AND took Plan B

#25.

come on guys

#11.

what
it's a possibility
it's a definite possibility

#13.

are we talking about 2 months ago?
when Dan came home for Thanksgiving?

#25.

yeah

#13.

no guys that was definitely Plan B

#2.

how do you know

#13.

Miss Armenia told me
…guys we cannot go around telling people she got an abortion

#2.

what's Plan B?

> **#14** *and* **#7** *jog in*
> **#14** *holds something behind her back*

#2.

guys? what's / Plan

#25.	**#13.**	**#11.**
look who's back!	yo yo!	hey guys!

#8.

OH
Hi
hello

#7.

were you guys talking about us or something?

#13.

    uh

    nope

#8.

    hahahaha

    hahahaha

#11.

    there's a bird in the air dome

#7.

    what-ever

    big news guys:

#14.

    my mom brought orange slices

        she tosses orange slices into the group

        they stop stretching and descend on the Ziploc bag

#13.

    orange slices! dude!

#8.

    omigosh

#2.

    your mom's the best

#7.

    (sarcastic)

    she's like the Total Best

#14.

    ha totally

#8.

    orange slices!

    that's so so fun!

    guys remember when

#11.

    yes we all remember orange slices

#13.

    oh god

    they're delicious

#25.

    don't eat too many ladies

    no side cramps out there

#13.

    hey guys look

        #13 puts orange slice in mouth and smiles

#8.

    guys we used to do this all the time!

    oh my god

        #8 puts orange slice in mouth and smiles

#11.

    ha that rules

        #11 puts orange slice in mouth and smiles

#8.

    (orange slice in mouth)

    (you gotta do it)

        #8 holds an orange slice out to #2

#2.

    oh

    um

#8.

    (come on come on)

        #2 hesitates for a sec then puts orange slice in mouth and smiles
        she looks super stressed out
        #7 and #14 join in

#13.

    (my dudes I've got braces) #11.

                        (this tastes funny after a while)

#13.

    (look I'm 12 years old) #8.   #7.

                   (isn't this super fun)   **(wow)** #14.

                                                     (haha

#13.   **haha**

    (I've got braces)   **haha)**

#25.

    um girls

#14.

    (takes out orange slice)

    WAIT

    we should take a picture

    does anyone have their phone

    mine's dead

#11.

    (no)

#8.

   (yay! picture!)

#13.

   (in my backpack)

#14.

   what?

#13.

   (takes out orange slice)
   in my backpack
   the tie dye one
   on the bench

#14.

   cool

      #14 jogs off to the bench

#25.

   girls we should really finish

                        #11.

#8.   **(you know**

   (come on   **you want**

   for the picture)   **to)**

       #25 puts in a slice

#13.

   NO THE OTHER TIE DYE ONE
   THE TURQUOISE-Y ONE

      #00 jogs on and clocks the situation
      she puts in a slice

#13.

   IT'S IN THE BIG POCKET
   NO THE OTHER BIG
   YEAH NEXT TO MY INHALER?
   BINGO BANGO MY FRIEND

      #14 jogs back on with iPhone

#14.

   kay everybody um
   do something crazy

      they all pose in awesome ways except #46

#2.

   (I don't have one)

#7.

   (seriously?)

#2.

   (I'm not allowed)

#7.

   (um why?)

#2.

   (nodding)
   (radiation)

#7.

   (what?)

#2.

   (radiation?)

#7.

   (what?)

#2.

   (takes out slice)
   radiation!   #11.

                (radiation?)

#8.

   (yay!
   guys!
   let's all pose!
   let's pose like Charlie's Angels)

      (takes out slice)
   LET'S POSE LIKE CHARLIE'S ANGELS

#7.

   (um, no
   let's just like do whatever)

#8.

   (disappointed)
   ok

#25.

> *(takes out orange slice)*
> hey
> wanna get in the picture?

#46.

> *(on verge of tears)*
> I don't get it

#25.

> what?

#46.

> why do they have orange peels in their mouths?

>> *they all stare at her in shock with orange peels in their mouths*

#25.

> wow
> uh
> just do it ok?

>> **#46** *puts an orange in and gets in the picture*

#14.

> alright
> um
> look fierce

>> **#14** *takes the photo with an iPhone.*

> very cool you guys

>> *they spit them out and crowd around the iPhone*

#7.	**#13.**	**#11.**
can I see?	did you use the filter	oranges are so good you guys

#8.

> wait we should do a goofy one
> guys can we do a goofy one

>> **#2** *cleans off her tongue*

#13.

> *(looking at it)*
> very nice
> want me to take one with you in it?

>> *whistle*

#25.

> alright that's game
> let's get out there ladies!
> hustle!
> someone grab the slices!   **#2.**
>
>>   I'll get 'em   **#13.**

#25.

>>   Fusion is going downnnntownnn

> let's go let's go

#7.

time to climb The Wall

#13.

more like *(monster voice)* DESTROY IT

#14.

(to #00)
hey my ACL's acting up
can I use your wrap

#00 *nods*

#25.

how's it feeling

#14.

you know

#11.

can I have some too?

#25 *jogs off with* **#00,** **#14,** *and* **#11**

#8.

hey do you think they play soccer?

#13.

who?

#8.

all the immigrant kids
do you think someone gives them like mini soccer balls?

#7.

jesus christ

#8.

what?
what?

#13.

muy muy muy racista

#8, **#7,** **#13** *jog off*
#2 *picks up the orange slices and looks at* **#46,** *who looks up*

#2.

hey um

#46.

the tufted titmouse is still there

#2.

oh cool

#46.

but now I'm thinking it's more of a bushtit

#2.

oh
that's good
…um

#2.

I just wanted to
I wanted to say
it's so nice you're trying a new sport

#46.

…thanks

#2.

I mean it must be hard
to move somewhere?
and not know anyone?
…
I guess what I mean is I'm
…
I'm sorry I said you lived in a yogurt

#46.

right

#2.

I think it's neat
…a yurt sounds pretty neat

> **#46** *stares at her for a sec*
> *and jogs off*
> **#2** *devours the entire bag of orange slices*
> *whistle*

WEEK THREE – MARTIN LUTHER KING JR. DAY

the field is empty

#25.

HIGH KNEES

the whole team runs past doing high knees
a few seconds – they run past again

#25.

BUTT KICKS

they run past doing butt kicks
a few seconds – they run past again

#25.

HIGH KNEES/BUTT KICKS

they run past doing high knees/butt kicks
a few seconds – they run past again

#25.

GRAPEVINE

they run past doing grapevine
a few seconds – they run past again

#25.

ALRIGHT COME IN
COME IN

#11.*

(winded)
jesus she's working us

#7.

(winded)
cause we fucking lost

#14.

(winded)
to fucking Fusion

#13.

(winded)
never again guys
never again

#11 *is coughing*

#2.

(winded)
are you ok?

#11.

(winded)
yeah totally

> **#25** *carries a mesh bag of soccer balls*
> *she empties it*

#25.

ALRIGHT ALRIGHT
LET'S HUSTLE

---

* **#11** and **#00** have a cold this week

#25.

    BIG GAME TODAY
    AND IT'S NOT GOING TO WIN ITSELF

#13.

    Blue Storm is going downnn

#7.

    bitches won't know what hit 'em

#25.

    PARTNER UP

        #14 and #7 pair up immediately

#25.

    I WANT TO SEE TIGHT PASSES
    SOFT TOUCHES
    INSIDE OUTSIDE
    LEFT RIGHT
    HUSTLE LADIES

          #2.
          (to #13)
          partner?

#25.

I WANT US LOOKING GOOD OUT THERE TODAY

          #13.
          (detective-y)
          sure thing sweetheart

#25.

    (to #00)
    ready?

        #00 nods and puts on her gloves

          #2.
          (confused by reference)
          …ok

#7.

    (to #14)
    did you bring your stuff?

#14.

    (innocent)
    what stuff?

#7.

    um like a bikini?
    a toothbrush?

#14.

    (overplaying)
    oh oops I like totally forgot

guess I'll just have to SKINNY DIP

#8.

god I hope we win

#7.

(with love and delight)
you total fucking slut!

#11.

we have to
we have to beat them

#8.

(sigh of longing)
Miami

#11.

they went to Epcot
you know?
Epcot
in a limo
with like discounted tickets

#8.

it's so unfair

#11.

and our final game
last spring
all-district tournament
was like SO CLOSE

#8.

I know

#46 *approaches them*

#46.

hey um
mind if I join?

#11.

oh
uh
ok
sure
sure

#13.

sick headgear bra

#2 *is wearing a protective headband*

#11.

we'll make it a triangle

#2.

I hate it
my mom's making me wear it
she bought it on amazon

#13.

cause of last week

#2.

yeah apparently I got another concussion or something

#13.

oh mannnn
this is number?

#2.

5 I think
no no
6

#13.

you're like Queen of the CAT scan

#2.

yeah my mom's like "thank god we have insurance now" but

	#25.
#13.	*(to #00)*
yo!	quick hands
we should get you like a kitty tiara!	
#2.	**#25.**
what?	*(to #00)*
	quick hands
#13.	
(British accent)	
"Queen of the CAT Scan"	
#2.	
oh!	
that's funny	**#25.**
	(to #00)
	there we go
#13.	that's more like it
meow meow	

#2.

(not quite a British accent)
"Queen of the CAT Scan"

they're both a little embarrassed about her bad accent

#13.

your mom was freaking out

#2.

my mom was totally freaking

#13.

    it was a sick header though

#2.

    right?

           #7.

               I am so fucking pumped

           #14.

               yeah Martin Luther King Jr. Day is like totally my favorite holiday

           #7.

               shut up asshole

           #14.

               oh right
               and it's your birthday

           #7.

               oh right
               and we're going to my dad's ski house
               and that asshole won't be there
               and he has like a fully stocked bar

#46.

    (off)
    sorry

      she runs across

#8.

    (off)
    it's ok

           #7.

               so shut the fuck up you ungrateful whore

      #8 *and* **#11** *wait for her to bring the ball*

#11.

    …
    …
    have you heard about diedinhouse.com

#8.

    what

#11.

    diedinhouse.com
    it's a service
    you pay them and they tell you if anyone has died in your house

#8.

    how do you find this stuff
    that is so scary

#11.

    just the internet

#8.

but you have to search for something like that
why would you search for

#11.

no it was like on
like on my Gmail
like an ad
or on Facebook or something
I don't know

> **#46** *walks back on with ball and stands behind* **#8**

#8.

so creepy

#46.

what is?

#8.

OMIGOSH
omigosh
omigosh you scared me

#11.

diedinhouse.com
it like tells you if someone died in your house or something

#46.

someone died in my house

> *slight pause*

#11.

who

#46.

I don't know
he won't tell me his name

#8.

Oh
My
Gosh

#11.

…don't you mean your yurt?

> **#13.**
>
> I hear a scout's coming for Jordana today
>
> **#2.**
>
> what?
>
> **#13.**
>
> yep Jordana Frye

#2.

really?

#13.

yep yep

#2.

crap

…

…

she's so good

#13.

I know

#7.

OW

#14.

what

#7.

I forgot how much these hurt

#14.

what?

#7.

I just got waxed

#14.

ohhh

#7.

owwww

#00.

ACHOO

#14.

I can't believe you do that
it must be like so painful

#7.

I guess

#25.

are you sick?

#14.

my sister says it's like bitchslapping your vagina
but with hot oil
like a hot oil bitchslap

#25.

goddammit

#7.

I have a pretty high pain tolerance so

#14.

wait is Dan coming this weekend?

#7.

it's my birthday so like he better fucking come

#14.

and you didn't invite anyone else?

#7.

well Dan's bringing a friend

#14.

(uncomfortable)
so it's just you and Dan
and me and like some college guy I don't know

#7.

chill the fuck
kay
he's hot
we'll ski
we'll go in the jacuzzi
Dan'll make his famous screwdrivers
it'll be crazy
kay?

#14.

kay

>
>
> **#8.**
>
> *(off)*
> WAIT

#14.

how hot

>
>
>
> **#11.**
>
> so some guy died in your yurt?
> and he like haunts it?
>
> **#46.**
>
> perhaps
>
> **#8.**
>
> omigosh you guys I am so scared
>
> **#11.**
>
> how do you know it's a spirit
> what if it's just a drafty window
>
> **#46.**
>
> yurts don't have windows
>
> **#8.**
>
> or like
> like a door
> do you have a door?

#25.

LADIES!
COME IN!

#11.

of course she has a door
how else would she get inside the yurt

#8.

I don't know
I do not know

#25.

COME IN

#8.

...with a spoon?

they giggle like only 16-year-olds can

#25.

what's so funny

#11.

(laughing)
"with a spoon"

#8.

(laughing)
"how else? with a spoon"

#25.

Ladies

#11.

(laughing)
cause
cause yogurt
you know

#2.

#8.   when we get scholarships
(laughing)   do you think they'll be full-ride?
"with a spoon"

#11.	#13.	#7.
oh man	uh	(plus they're just a bunch of
sorry	those are pretty rare	dumb virgins)

#8.   **#14.**
whoo   hahaha

#11.   **#2.**
phew   right   **#7.**
                                                  (or like
#8.   secret lesbians)
spoon

#11.   **#2.**   **#14.**
spoon   right   hahahaha

> #46 *intercepts their pass*
> *she juggles their ball*
> *she is amazing*

#46.

(chants)
I LIVE IN A YOGURT
MY FEELINGS DON'T GET HURT
YOGURT FOR BREAKFAST
YOGURT FOR LUNCH
I LIVE IN A YOGURT
MY FEELINGS DON'T GET HURT
YOGURT FOR DINNER
YOGURT FOR BRUNCH
I LIVE IN A YOGURT
MY FEELINGS DON'T GET HURT
YOGURT FOR SNACK
YOGURT FOR SNACKY SNACKY
I LIVE IN A YOGURT
MY FEELINGS DON'T GET HURT
YOGURT FOR DESSERT
YOGURT FOR

> *she drops the ball*
> *everyone is watching*

#2.

wow

> #46 *sprints off*

#11.

what was that?

#13.

seriously yo

#2.

do you think she's ok?

#25.

LADIES
…
just
…
team work makes the dream work
you know?

> #25 *jogs off*

#25.

(off)
GODDAMMIT KEEP PASSING

#14.

that was interesting

#8.

so weird
but so good at that

#7.

if only she could play like center whatever

pause

#13.

you guys she sounds exactly like

#8.

oh my gosh

#7.

"mark your man goddammit"

#14.

"if you let another goddamn ball in"

#11.

"that's it goddammit we're running laps"

#13.

wow wow wow
Frankie Jr.
here in da flesh

#00.

"I live in a yogurt"

everyone stares at her

#00.

…it's catchy

#00 *runs off to vomit*

#8.

can I just say
I just don't get what the big deal is about like self-knowledge

#11.

…what?

#8.

like
what's the big deal
there are so many other things to know about
why waste time knowing about yourself

#7.

…where is this coming from?

#8.

oh
I went over to Chris's house
and he was like
all moody and talking about self-knowledge

#13.

total downer

#14.

he's cute

#2.

in like a scary way

#8.

yeah
I don't know
he like made fun of my calf muscles
and tried to stick his hand down my shirt

#7.

cool

#8.

um not really

pause

#7.

let's do the spiderweb?

#13.

righteous

#2.

yay!

#14.

yeah

#8.

ooh I love the spiderweb

*they do the spiderweb
it's a complicated, interwoven passing drill
it's pretty impressive actually*

#2.

did you guys hear a scout's coming?

#11.

really?

#13.

for Jordana Frye

#7.

shit

#14.

from where?

#13.

I mean I think she's getting scouted by like everyone
but I think Santa Barbara

#2.

Santa Barbara?
you didn't tell me that

#7.

shit

#14.

that's like the best team

#8.

but the showcase tournament isn't until next week

#13.

I know they must just want like early dibs you know

#11.

is that even legal? like NCAA approved legal?

#8.

have you guys emailed coaches yet?
I get so nervous I never know how to start it

#7.

um "dear coach"

#8.

yeah but like I don't know
it just makes me nervous
what if there's like a spelling error or I say the wrong thing
or like the wrong tone

#13.

you gotta chill my man

#11.

wait how'd you hear that?

#13.

what?

#11.

about the scout?

#13.

oh uh dunno
guess Coach told me

#11.

Coach?

#13.

yep

#8.

wait you mean like Coach Neil?
like Neil Neil?

#14.

the creep who asked us to scrimmage in our sports bras?

#8.

ew

#2.

I hated that

#7.

he's totally hungover again

#2.

he is?

they all look off

#11.

thus Coach Frankie Jr.

#7.

which is total bullshit

#2.

you guys she's doing her best

#7.

we're paying out the ass for a coach

#11.

our parents are paying out the ass for a coach

#7.

still a fucking rip-off
Tony would never do this to boy's U17 indoor

#8.

I can't believe they got Coach Mikhail

#2.

he played in Croatia right?
like on a pro team?

#11.

I thought Czech Republic

#8.

he is so scary

#13.

I think he killed a man once
in like… *(scary voice)* the 80s

#14.

I think he's sorta sexy

#8.

he's like 45!!

#14.

so's Jude Law

#8.

so's my dad

#7.

we should get fucking Coach Mikhail!
not this washed-up pudgeball who spends games at the vending machine

#13.

hey he really wanted that pop-tart

#7.

it's like
it's like sexist

that's what this is
sexist

#2.

c'mon it's just indoor

#7.

just indoor?
we're juniors
this spring is what counts if we wanna play college

#2.

I know I know but like
you know

#7.

no
I don't fucking know

>   **#00** *comes back and does private goalie drills*
>   *but she's listening*

#8.

wow you are such a feminist

#7.

what?
no
it's not about
I'm just like
it's just like fucked up you know?

#11.

I'm a feminist
what's wrong with being a feminist

#14.

guys look
he literally fell asleep

>   *they look at him*

#11.

I just can't believe that Neil is in the Army

#8.

really?

#2.

I thought he worked at like RadioShack

#13.

Best Buy yo

#11.

he's National Guard
remember his stupid story about the humvee

#8.

oh yeah didn't he like go to Iraq?

#13.

Afghanistan

#7.

    if he's America's best
    America is sorely fucked

#11.

    guys what if Neil did like
    Abu Ghraib shit?

#8.

    Abu what?

#11.

    oh come on you know about Abu Ghraib

#8.

    um no

#11.

    like torture in prison

#2.

    in Afghanistan

#7.

    no like Iraq

#11.

    yeah definitely Iraq   **#14.**

                                              …definitely

#7.

    those pictures of the guys with bags over their head
    like naked standing on boxes

#8.

    ugh

#2.

    we saw pictures in Amnesty International

#11.

    I heard they'd like
    the like female guards would like
    would like you know

#8.

    like what

#11.

    like (arouse them)

#2.

    what?

#11.

    (nods)
    like take off their shirts
    and you know

#8.

ew with like terrorists?

#14.

I heard about that

#2.

why?

#13.

guys Neil did not torture terrorists with his titties

#7.

oh yeah?
how would you know?

#8.

I miss Coach Patrick

#2.

yeah

#14.

I know

#8.

I love Coach Patrick

#11.

can't believe he's in Idaho

#2.

we should send him a card or something

#14.

we should like text him that orange slice pic
as like a "get-well" thing

#7.

for him or for his mom?

#8.

it's so amazing he moved home

#14.

what's wrong with her again?

#11.

I think she has terminal breast cancer?

#14.

oh right

#13.

yeah
like stage 4 right?

#8.

I hope he's back by March
I do not want Coach Creep for travel team

#13.

you realize that means you want his mom to croak

#8.

what??

#13.

cause that's the only way he's moving back
is if his mom you know

#2.

that's an awful thing to say

#13.

I mean
would you rather have Coach Patrick's mom die from breast cancer
OR
have Neil for travel team?

#8.

…um

#13.

are you hesitating??

#8.   #7.

no I mean   wow

#8.   #14.   #11.

no   WOW   that's nuts
guys!

#7.

that is some intense shit

#13.

she's just a sweet old lady with one titty!   #11.

                                                      what's with you and titties today?

#8.

guys come on
I just like hate Coach Neil

#7.

hate him enough to kill Coach Patrick's mom?

                                                      #2.

#8.   guys?

(getting upset)
oh my gosh you guys

#11.

yeah but you don't NOT want to kill his mother   #2.

                                                         hey you guys?

#7.

exactly

#13.

girl wants mommy to die of the big C

#8.

> (on verge of tears)
> I DO NOT!!
> Take it back!!

#13.

> what?

#8.

> you're not allowed to say that!!
> take it back!!

#13.

> ok!!
> jesus!
> I take it back!!
> it is taken back!!

> *#8 is super upset*

#13.

> oh
> shit
> your mom   **#11.**
> I forgot   yeah   **#7.**
> I'm sorry   sorry   yikes
> ...shit   **#14.**
>   yeah

#8.

> (still really upset)
> ...it's fine

#2.

> are you ok?

#8.

> I'm great

> *awkward pause*

#7.

> soooo
> who has plans for the three day weekend?

#11.

> homework
> lots and lots of homework

#2.

> I'm doing a day of service at Wingfield Park
> you guys should come!

#11.

> how do you have time?

#2.

already finished my paper on Rwanda

#11.

seriously?
you suck

#8.

(chipper)
hey isn't it almost someone's birthday??

#11.

(to #7)
right! January 19

#8.

birthstone: garnet

#7.

what?

#8.

remember? the birthstone club?

#11.

party tonight or Sunday?

#2.

yeah when's it /

#7.

oh I'm actually just like
hanging with Dan
at my dad's ski house

#8.

you're not having a party this year?

#7.

nah
too old for like slumber parties

#2.

but you always have a slumber party

#7.

yeah
yeah

#8.

WELL
my stepmom said I could have some people over
so if anyone wants to sleep over Sunday?
we can like watch a movie?

#13.

(to #8)
hey
that was like
major FOOT in MOUTH

#2.

happy birthday!

#11.

oh

#11.

> definitely
>
> free me from the tyranny of Sunday night dinners

#00 *nods*

#2.

> > I'll ask my mom

#13.

> want me to bring my laptop??

#8.

> *(to #14)*
> omigosh
> will you bring your iPad
> so we can watch Game of Thrones??

#14.

> um
> I'm like going out of town actually?
> with my family
> to like visit my cousins

#8.

> oh!
> the Armenians?

#14.

> ...the Americans

#8.

> does anyone else have HBO GO?

#13.

> I have HBO GO!!

#2.

> that sounds nice

#11.

> we could ask Stephanie
> are you inviting Stephanie?

#8.

> yeah

#13.

> hey I have HBO GO

#8.

> *(sorta displeased)*
> cool

#13.

> coolio!
> I'll bring my laptop

#11.

> also guys:
> guess what our fine captain is up to this weekend

#7.

> taking a fucking chill pill

> > *laughter*

#11.

> hanging out with –

#11.

drumroll please –
Louise

#7.

who?

#14.

yeah who?

#13.

no

#11.

yes

#8.

weird new girl at our school
she licked the microphone

#13.

Louise Peterson?

#7.

she did what?

#25 and #46 jog back in
#25 is so stressed

#8.

omigosh
why

#11.

shhhh

#13.

shut up

#25.

ALRIGHT
LET'S CIRCLE UP

they circle up

#8.

(wait why is she hanging out with Louise)

#11.

(exactly)

#25.

OK LADIES
So
Big Game Today
Great practice for the college showcase tournament / next week

#7.

/ we're not going to stretch?

#25.

no time

#7.

um hello that is like so fucking dangerous

#14.

yeah

#11.

yeah the doctor said

#25.

we don't have time ok
WE DON'T HAVE TIME

#7 and #14 exchange a look

#25.

ok you know what?
Everyone stretch
right now
yeah

they do

#25.

yeah
ok
great
So
Let's talk about last week
we lost last week
Right
Yeah
We Did   **#7.**
to a team that was worse than we were   (is this like her motivational speech?)
Why?
Cause we weren't listening to each other   **#14.**
(to #7 and #14.) I'm sorry Am I Interrupting??   (oy)

#7.

nope

#25.

Good
Now
This week
We're playing a good team

#13.

BLUE STORMMMMM

#25.

but we've beat them before

#11.

like 5 years ago

#13.

or as I like to call it
Phase Training Bra

#25.

Ok
So
We know they're good
and sure
they are
they're really good

#25.

they went to nationals last year right?
but are we scared?

      #7 and #14 roll their eyes
I said
Are We Scared?

#2.

(super loud)
NO!!

#25.

that's right
we're not scared
We're Ready to Play

#2.

WE'RE READY!!

#25.

cause This isn't about Last Year's Nationals
This isn't about Next Year's Nationals
This is about Right Here
Right Now
in City Sports Dome
so
…expect lots of shots on goal
which means mark your man
watch for breakaways
we're gonna play 2-2-1
I want 8 and me on D
14 and 11 in midfield

      to #14 and #8

#25.

but I want you guys to hang back play safe

#14.	**#8.**
gotcha	yep

#25.

and 46 as striker

#7.

…what?

#25.

(ignoring)
7 and 13 we'll sub you in fast
it's going to be a running game
so we'll be switching it / up constantly

#7.

the fuck are you talking about

#25.

they're really going to run us out there
and everybody watch / for Jordana

#7.

we're playing the best team in the league
in the fucking district
and you bench me?

#25.

hey this is all coming from Coach

#7.

give it a fucking break

#25.

language

#7.

she can't even kick the fucking ball straight!

#25.

HEY
we're a team
you wanna play?
you play With Us
All of Us
kay?

#7.

(salutes)
Yes Sir

       slight pause

#13.

did you hear a scout's coming today

#8.

yeah UC Santa Barbara

#11.

for Jordana

#25.

UC Santa Barbara?

#13.

yep yep

#25.

but tournament is a week away

#13.

I know

#13.

they're just like
early bird gets the worm ya know

>*slight pause*

#25.

Ladies
get that outta your head
and leave it off the field
Alright?

#2.

YEAH!

#25.

Now Let's Push Ourselves Today
Push Further Than You Think You Can
And Keep On Pushing
cause I don't know about you
But goddammit I Want to Win

#8.

kick some Blue Storm booty!

#13.

ow ow!

#2.

let's freaking kill 'em!

#11.

let's do it

>*whistle*

#25.

that's kick-off
let's cheer and get out there

>*they huddle up real tight, heads down*
>*we hear whispers of "we are the wolves we are the"*

#8.

AHHHHHH!

>**#8** *breaks the circle*

#14.

jesus

#8.

omigosh there's blood all over my jersey!!

#11.

(to #2) your nose is bleeding

#2.

what?

>**#2** *has a nosebleed*

#14.

    jesus it's like gushing blood

        #2 *touches it and looks at her finger*
        whistle

WEEK FOUR – THE CAMBODIAN II

seven girls in uniform run in from the cold
they're sweaty and pumped up and dusted with snow

#8.*

omigosh it is freezing out there!!!

#13.*

whoo yeah

> **#13** *puffs on inhaler*

#2.*

I can't feel my ears

#11.

it's cold as shit

#2.

can you guys feel your ears?

#8.

what's the point of doing a warm-up run
outside
when it's snowing?

#25.*

keeps the blood pumping

#11.

I mean it's also a cool-down
technically

#2.

how many more today?
I feel icky

#8.

one more

#11.

at least

#25.

ALRIGHT LADIES
great game

#8.

woo woo!

#14.

colder than a witch's tit

#13.

(exhales inhaler)
um
what?

#14.

what?

#13.

a witch's tit?

#14.

um
yeah?

#13.

are witch's tits
like
particularly cold?

#13.

we were on fi-yahhhhhhh

#11.

SHE was on fire

---

* **#8** and **#25** and **#2** and **#13** have a cold this week

#25.

yeah yeah we looked good today
but we've got another one in 30
so let's hydrate
and circle up

#13.

college showcase tour-na-MENT

they circle up and start the warm-up

#13.

shit guys
shit
can I just say
that was
So Sick

#11.

completely nuts

#8.

omigosh she's so good

#2.

I've never seen anyone play like that
even in like the World Cup

#14.

who knew?

#11.

I mean she was pretty good last
week

#14.

she's been holding out on us

#25.

that bicycle kick

#13.

not like this man

#8.

and like in front of all of
these scouts??

#2.

wait where'd she go?

*#7 walks in on crutches with a boot
she's in street clothes with a team hoodie and a Frappuccino
she has a ski goggle tan, and so does #14*

#7.

what's up sluts

#14 rolls her eyes

#8.

omigosh hey! **#2.**

hi! **#11.**

heard you cheering out there **#13.**

"fucking kill 'em"

#7.

haha yeah
you guys were fucking great

#2.

thanks!

#7.

nice helmet

#2 is wearing even bigger headgear

#2.

(blushes)
my mom

#11.

cause of the nosebleeds?

#2 nods

#13.

sweet ride dude

#7.

fuck you
my armpits are killing me

#13.

ha ha

#8.

how's it feeling?

#7.

you know
like super shitty

#11.

oof that sucks

#8 blows air through lips

#7.

but I have a pretty high pain tolerance so

#14 rolls her eyes

#25.

what'd the doctor say?

#7.

torn ACL

collective sigh

#13.

shit dude

#11.

aw man
it didn't look that bad on the field

#8.

I thought it was a sprain at most

#7.

yeah well guess not

#2.

what a lousy birthday present

#7.

haha yeah

#13.

"happy 17!

here, have a bum knee for the REST OF YOUR / ADULT LIFE"

#11.

/ shhhh

#2.

do you need surgery?

#7.

looks like it

collective sigh

#11.

it's not so bad
I was back on the field in a couple of months

#7.

yeah

#8.

but that was what
like U14

#11.

U12 but still

#2.

(to #14)
and it only took you like 10 weeks
last season
right?

#14.

(to #2)
yeah
but it was a less serious injury

#7.

lucky bitch

#14.

(biting)
yep
and I took really good care of it

slight pause

#7.

yeah
it pretty much fucking blows
but they say maybe I'll be back in time for travel team

#2.

this spring?
that's / great

#7.

no

#7.

uh
fall

#2.

oh

slight pause where they all feel bad

#7.

maybe I can make an ID camp though

#8.

cool!   **#2.**

cool   that's so great   **#13.**

rad man

#7.

yeah the Ohio one's not till August
and they're in my top 10

#11.

great program at Ohio

#13.

for sure

#7.

yeah
as long as I rehab fast
you know

#2.

totally

#13.

fingers crossed man

#25.

well thanks for coming out today

#7.

got nothing else to do with my fucking Saturdays

laughter

#7.

when's the next game?

#25.

30 minutes or so

#7.

the Diablos?

#11.   **#25.**

that's tomorrow I think   tomorrow
                                                 9 a.m.   **#13.**

#2.   ack!
                                                                               9 a.m.?
we're playing Xtreme Xplosion
                                                                               that's like my primo REM cycle

#7.

oh you'll fucking destroy them

#11.

hope so

#25.

let's not get cocky

#7.

strong on D but terrible shots

#25.

yeah really strong D

#13.

it was a pretty sweet side tackle

#7.

thanks

#25.

you shouldn't have kept playing on it
after that

#7.

whatever
pain is a state of mind
you know

> **#14** *rolls her eyes*

#25.

ok but I told you
it could have prevented surgery

#7.

and I told you we should have stretched
but
can't win 'em all I guess

> *pause*

#7.

but we beat 'em!
we beat Blue Storm!
next stop nationals!

#13.

"I'm in Miami bitch"

#8.

(sigh)
Miami
oh my gosh do I want to go to Miami

#11.

the look on Jordana Frye's face when the ref blew the whistle

#13.

ah ha ha ha

#11.

 priceless

#2.

 it felt good

#7.

 hell yeah it felt good

#25.

 it's just indoor
 doesn't count / for

#7.

 whatever
 it's not ECNL play
 but still
 it fucking rocked

#14.

 (points to #7)
 hey did you see that bicycle kick?

#8.

 omigosh

#13.

 so rad
 so super rad

#11.

 she's a beast

#7.

 (diffident)
 I guess

#14.

 who knew she'd be such a great striker?
 right?

#8.

 omigosh I know
 she scored like 5 goals!!
 who does that??

#7.

 ok but their goalie was a total joke

#14.

 I hate to say it
 but she's like
 totally giving you a run for your money

#7.

 ha thanks

#14.

I mean have you ever scored with a bicycle kick?

#7.

I mean I can do them

#14.

no you can't

#7.

um yes I fucking can

#14.

how come I've never seen it

#7.

I do it at home
when I practice at home

#14.

I bet it's like on your stupid fucking trampoline

#7.

uh
no

#14.

you're a fucking liar
it's on the trampoline

#7.

um chill the fuck out

#14.

ANYONE can do it on the fucking trampoline

#7.

I can DO a fucking bicycle kick

#14.

then PROVE IT you CUNT

> *a shocked pause from all*
> **#46** *walks in*
> *she's happier than we've ever seen her*

#46.

hi guys!
great game right?
(to #7)
oh! hey!
/ you made it!

#7.

(to #14)
/ what the fuck is wrong with you

#14.

nothing

#7.

uh ok

#14.

I just don't have time for liars anymore
you know?

#25.

HEY
I don't know what's going on but /

#7.

/ oh fuck you
you're not our coach
and you're a shitty / captain

#46.

(to #25) um

#25.

/ and you're not playing this game
so I suggest you get off the field

#14.

yeah
get off the fucking / field

#7.

/ you're such a prude

#14.

am not

#46.

um Captain

#7.

that's not what Brendan said

#14.

shut up

#7.

it was just a fucking b / lowjob

#14.

(panicked)
shut up
SHUT UP

#46.

um
uh
Captain?
I think Coach wants to see you

all look off

#2.

who's that guy with Coach?

#8.

I saw him on the sidelines
taking notes

#13.

wait is he

#25.

> hydrate ladies hydrate

>> *#25 jogs off*
>> *they all keep staring*

#11.

> guys
> he's wearing a suit

>> *silence*
>> *they watch* **#25** *talk to Coach and the man in the suit*

#00.

> shit

>> *#25 jogs back on*

#13.

> from what school?
> did he say?

#8.

> Santa Barbara?
> was it Santa Barbara?

#2.

> I bet Stanford

#11.

> maybe Bucknell
> I invited Bucknell

#25.

> ladies ladies
> coach wants to see #14, #46, and #00

>> *loaded pause*

#25.

> go on
> hustle

#14.

> kay

>> *#14, #46, #00 jog off*
>> *#46 does a weird wave*
>> *slight pause*

#7.

> fuck

#25.

> hey

#13.

> he's a scout
> right
> he has to be a scout

#25.

> I don't know

#7.

> bullshit

#25.

    I don't know

#7.

    you just shook his hand!

#11.

    his clipboard says Texas A&M
    so I'm guessing he's from Texas A&M

        pause

#7.

    shoulda been out there

#25.

    shoulda stopped playing when I told you to

#7.

    shoulda stretched before I played
    …fuck

#8.

    …maybe they'll just call us over in small groups
    so we can like meet him individually?

#13.

    sure
    sure
    maybe my face will turn into a walrus face

    #13 *makes a walrus face*

#2.

    do you guys think I played ok today?

#8.

    (to #13)
    quit it

    #13 *does a vulgar walrus*

#8.

    I said quit it!

#25.

    you did
    we all did

#7.

    you were great

#11.

    you did miss that shot

#2.

    which shot?

#11.

    my corner kick

#2.

    it was too high
    I couldn't get to it

#11.

    no it wasn't
    maybe if you weren't so scared of getting another concussion

#2.

    it was too high

#25.

    hey we all played like champs today

        they all look off

#7.

    I've been playing for like 13 years
    and she just fucking picked it up

#11.

    yeah
    this is her first season
    like ever

#8.

    that's like so impossible

#7.

    there's no fucking way

#25.

    Ladies

#11.

    where'd she even move from again?

#13.

    she never told us
    dude she never told us

#8.

    I bet she like played travel
    or like O.D.P.
    and just isn't saying

#7.

    you don't learn to play like that
    in just a couple weeks of indoor

#13.

    she totally played O.D.P.

#2.

    (upset)
    and she's SO STINKY!

#8.

    (to #25)
    I mean I just like can't believe he didn't want you

#25.

    what?

#8.

    I mean I can't believe you're not over there
    you're like so good

#8.

    and you like work so hard

#11.

    yeah seriously

#13.

    si si señor es pollo loco

#8.

    (looking off)
    they're laughing
    they're all laughing

        they all look

#2.

    (looking off)
    what are they writing down

#8.

    oh my god
    did he sign them?
    what if he signed them?

#7.

    don't be a moron
    he wouldn't sign them right now
    Dan had like a whole waiting period

#13.

    he probably just got their phone numbers

#11.

    oh my god
    she's going to vomit

#13.

    no

#8.

    omigosh

#7.

    she's going to hurl all over his clipboard

#2.

    hold it in!
    hold it in

#11.

    she's keeping it together

#13.

    it's staying down

#7.

    they're shaking hands again

#8.

omigosh

> **#46, #14, #00** *jog back on*

#11.

how was it?

#8.

what'd they say?

> **#00** *runs off to vomit*

#13.

thar she blows!

#11.

c'mon c'mon
tell us the good stuff

#46.

he was very nice

#14.

he just wanted our phone numbers
and like emails

#13.

cool
cool

#2.

where's he from?

#46.

um Texas A&M?
I think?

#7.

(she thinks)

#14.

yeah
Texas A&M

#11.

(furious)
…that's so fun!

#46.

…yeah!

#14.

(to #46, directed at #7)
you should tell them what he told you

#8.

what
omigosh what

#46.

oh nothing

#14.

> *(to #7)*
> she's being modest
> he was like
> "that bicycle kick coulda been on ESPN"

#46.

> haha
> yeah

#7.

> …you've played soccer before
> right?

#46.

> what do you mean?

#13.

> did you play O.D.P?

#46.

> O.D.P?

#11.

> Olympic Development Program

#8.

> like there's no way this is your first time on a team
> there's like SO no way

#46.

> *(laughing a little)*
> no
> the Olympics?
> definitely not
> this is actually my first team
> with like jerseys

#13.

> *(suspicious)*
> really dude?

#46.

> yes

#11.

> but that's
> you're so

#2.

> good

#46.

> oh I mean but I've played before
> I've played a lot

#2.

where?

#46.

uh well

all over the world actually

#13.

WHAAAAAAT??

#46.

yeah

my mom travels a lot for her job so

we move uh

pretty much constantly

#14.

whoa

#46.

and everyone plays football

um soccer

like everywhere

like Jakarta Krakow La Paz uh Kampala

even if you don't speak the language

so it's uh

it's a good way to uh

make

(self-conscious) friends

#11.

...wait what does your mom do?

#13.

does she like work for the CIA?

#8.

omigosh is your mom a spy??

#46.

haha

no

no

she's um

she's a travel writer

#11.

that's something you can actually be?

#46.

I guess so

not a lot of people do it

#8.

wait wait wait

#8.

    is she like famous??

#46.

    (shrugs)

    not unless you're really into travel writing

#11.

    so like where have you gone

#46.

    oh um all over

    we just got back from Morocco

    before that Cambodia

#13.

    you've been to Cambodia??

#46.

    yeah

    I um I think I told you that

#2.

    whoa

#13.

    holy shit man

    so like you know all about the *(mispronounces)* Khmer Rouge

	#11.
#46.	Khmer Rouge
(shrugs)	Khmer Rouge
sorta	

#7.

    wait if you've been to all these places

    then like why the fuck are you living here?

#46.

    oh

    my grandma lives here

    she's really sick

    she has emphysema?

#8.

    …oh my gosh

        #00 *walks back on*

#46.

    hey um

    sorry about your leg

#7.

it fucking sucks

#46.

you shoulda been out there today

#7.

I know

#46.

you're a really good striker

#7.

yeah
I know
…you looked good out there

#46.

(excited)
really?

#7.

(sorta aggressive)
yeah really

#46.

(a little moved)
thanks

#8.

I mean obviously duh you were so awesome

#46.

(to #7)
that means a lot
that's
thanks

#7.

whatever don't be weird about it

#8.

thank god you came back from Cambodia you know
that's all I gotta say
thank god

#46.

(to #7, familiar)
man you've had a rough couple of months huh?

#7.

what do you mean?

#2.

oh!

#11.

what?

#2.

I forgot
hold on

#2 jogs off

#46.

you know the uh   **#13** *coughs*
the um thing around Thanksgiving?

#7.

what?   **#8.**

#25.   **#11.**   that sounds great

ladies let's uh   yeah!   **#25.**
let's move on to passing   let's do it

#46.

it's just great that you have such a supportive boyfriend

#7.

the fuck you know about my boyfriend?
wait

              #7 *looks to* **#14**

#7.

are you fucking serious?

#14.

hey
no
that's not

#7.

it was just PLAN B you dicks

#14.   **#13.**

I didn't tell anyone I swear   (that's what I said)

#7.   **#11.**

you know what?   (shut up)
fuck you guys
fuck this
what I do with my body is my own fucking business
I don't need this
I quit

#14.

you're not going to fucking quit

#7.

you're right
I'm not
I fucking love soccer
maybe I'll just join BLUE STORM

#14.

fuck you

#7.

fuck YOU I invited YOU

and YOU moped like a little pussy

#14.

you LEFT ME ALONE with that guy

#7.

he LIKED you
and you said he was HOT

#14.

yeah but you just like
you abandoned me
to go FUCK your stupid FUCKING boyfriend!!
so / very LOUDLY!

#7.

/ I FUCKING LOVE HIM OK??
AND I NEVER GET TO SEE HIM!
/ EVER!

#14.

/ and then you SKIED on your fucking SPRAINED ANKLE

#7.

I HOPE YOU FUCKING ROT YOU MISERABLE

> **#2** *runs back on holding a scarf*

#2.

I made you a –

> *blackout*

TIME-OUT

#00 lies facedown in the middle of the field

the gymnasium is silent

a long while

she bolts up
her eyes are red
she spills open the bag of balls
she kicks each ball offstage in a fury

she is panting and wound up and crying

she tears her shirt off
and sinks to her knees

in a black sports bra
she holds her shirt
and screams

WEEK SIX – WE ARE THE WOLVES

> **#46** *sits in the middle of the field holding her phone*
> **#11** *stands at the edge wearing headphones*
> *they stare at each other*
> **#46** *sneezes**

#11.

...

...

...

hey

#46.

hey!

> **#11** *looks around and takes out her headphones*

#11.

have you been here?
long?

#46.

couple of minutes

#11.

...

...

#46.

really just got here

#11.

uh huh

#46.

...

#11.

...

#46.

...

#11.

...

#46.

how have you been
since the uh

#11.

good

#46.

...

---

* **#46** has a cold this week

#11.

   …

#46.

   good

#11.

   …
   well
   uh
   no
   I don't know
   I'm uh
   probably not good

#46.

   yeah
   yeah
   …
   probably not

#11.

   …

#46.

   …

#11.

   how about you

#46.

   oh
   you know

#46.

   …

#11.

   …

#46.

   I got the cold that was going around

#11.

   that sucks

#46.

   yeah
   it's ok

#11.

   want some Emergen-C?

#46.

   oh
   no

#11.

    it helps

#46.

    I think it's a placebo

#11.

    …

#46.

    …

#11.

    …

#46.

    so you think we have to forfeit?

#11.

    oh
    yeah
    I mean
    probably

#46.

    …

#11.

    …

#46.

    …

#46.

    I guess unless anyone else shows

#11.

    yeah

#46.

    we need six?

#11.

    six
    yeah

#46.

    cool

#11.

    …

#46.

    four to go!

#11.

    …

#46.

    …

#11.

...

#46.

...

have you uh

have you seen everyone

#11.

(nods)

at school and stuff

#46.

that's good

#11.

yeah

...

it's been weird

#46.

yeah

...

...

is everyone

uh

ok?

#11.

I uh I don't really

   #8 *walks on*

   she has a big zit

#8.

hi!

#46.

hey!

#11.

hey

#8.

um is anyone else here?

#11.

no

#8.

are we still on?

#11.

I don't know

#8.

alright

#8 *sighs and sits down*
#11 *is still standing*

#8.

so I guess now we're what
we're 5-2?

#46.

2?

#8.

Fusion and the forfeit

#11.

yeah

#46.

forfeit?

#11.

um last week?

#46.

oh

…

that counts?

#11.

I think so

pause

#8.

boo

pause

#8.

(texting)
people better get their asses out here

pause

#8.

(looks up)
can I just say
this is like so weird

#46.

yeah

#8.

it's like
really really weird

…

I keep crying?

…

I can't stop uh

#8.

but I do that all the time
so uh

pause

#11.

my dad keeps wanting to talk about it
like even in the car over here he was like
trying to talk about it
but I'm like
Not
Interested
I don't want to
I don't want to talk about it

#46.

huh

pause

#11.

I've talked about it

#8.

yeah

#11.

it's like
all I'm talking about

pause

#11.

especially when it's like
I'm driving
and he's like
trying to pump the break in the passenger seat
it just feels like
I don't know
like
…
disrespectful

pause

#11.

anyways

pause

#11.

I'm just like
could you be my dad for a sec and not my therapist?
you know?

#8.

  (checking her phone)
  that sucks

#46.

  wait I thought your mom was a therapist

#11.

  they're both therapists

#46.

  really?

#11.

  I don't wanna talk about it

          pause

#8.

  you got your permit?

#11.

  oh
  yeah

#8.

  lucky

#11.

  yeah
  it's um
  it's ok
  it's ok

          pause

#8.

  AHH!!

          they both look at her, concerned

#8.

  this zit is SO HUGE!

          pause

#8.

  it like hurts!
  you know when they like hurt?

#46.

  yeah

          pause

#8.

  I just want to like
  blast it off my face

          pause

#46.

it's not so bad

pause

#8.

it's huge

pause

#8.

I like stayed home from school yesterday cause it was so huge
I woke up and I was like nope

#8 picks her face
sighs

#8.

everyone else better show up

pause

#46.

how's Alex doing?

#11 and #8 exchange a look

#11.

she's uh
not great
you know

#46.

yeah

#8.

really not great

pause

#11.

Kristen told me she hasn't gone back to school since

#8.

yeah
I heard that too

#46.

who's Kristen?

#8.

(surprised)
omigosh you don't know Kristen?

#11.

oh she's on the travel team

#46.

there's more girls on the travel team?

#11.

    oh yeah

#8.

    loads more

#46.

    they don't play indoor?

#8.

    nah

    they have like other stuff you know

#46.

    like what

#11.

    um Kristen plays basketball for St. Albert

#8.

    and Mariana plays basketball for East High

#11.

    Emma P. and Jessica do ski team

#8.

    which is so dumb

    there are like so many injuries

#11.

    Taylor's recovering from surgery

#8.

    Ari's recovering from surgery

#11.

    Lily's recovering from surgery

#8.

    and Emma

    uh

    what's Emma doing?

#11.

    Emma P?

#8.

    no no Emma B.

#11.

    ohhh

    Emma B. wanted to be in the "school play"

        eye-roll

#8.

    how could I forget

#11.

    she plays like an old German guy

#11.

    a watchmaker or something

    (in accent) haven't you heard her German accent

#8.

    isn't she like Jewish?

#11.

    I know

    we sit together in calc

    and she keeps like whispering

    "don't you have ze guts to do vat you seenk ees right?"

#8.

    oh man

#11.

    she's so pumped

    she like gets to wear a moustache

#8.

    oh yeah I saw that on Instagram

#11.

    the biggest Instawhore

#46.

    I think I met her at the service

        pause

#8.

    I keep looking at that picture

    with the orange slices

#11.

    I can't

    it freaks me out too much

#8.

    I can't stop checking it

        #2 *and* **#00** *walk on*

#2.   **#00.**

    hey!   hi!

#8.

    oh great you made it

#11.

    hey guys

#2.

    yeah her mom gave me a ride

#00.

    wow

#2.

it's so good to see you guys

#00.

we almost have a full roster

#11.

yeah

wow

#00.

one more and we can play

according to regulations

#46.

that rocks

#00.

(to #46)

haven't seen you for a while

#46.

yeah

#2.

how've you been?

#46.

oh

it's been

yeah

sorta

sorta lonely

…

just sitting in my yurt uh

I uh

missed you guys

…

(to #00)

you're um

you're talking?

#00.

huh?

oh

yeah

ha

I guess I am

#11.

you feel ok?

#00.

I don't really know

I haven't thought about it

#8.

do you feel like you have to...?

#00.

no
no
I guess I uh
interesting
I think I don't feel as stressed?

#2.

about what

#00.

about like
like people scoring on me
missing the ball
seeing it pass through my fingers
or like penalty kicks
or like corner kicks
or a shoot-out even
or just like losing
losing the game
it's not
I visualize a lot
I'm pretty much always visualizing
during warm-ups
at night when I can't sleep
when I noodle around on the sax
but
it doesn't seem so...scary
right now
I guess

#11.

cool

#00.

or maybe I think we're gonna forfeit
so it just hasn't hit me yet
...
um so how are you guys?

#11.

ok

#8.

ok

#46.

yeah

pause

#2.

this is so weird

#8.

that's what I said
it's really weird being here

pause

#11.

she shouldn't have worn headphones

#8.

yeah but

#11.

she shouldn't have
it's so dangerous
she knew that

#00.

that guy should have scraped his windshield
or like defrosted it

#11.

right I know but if she had heard him?

#2.

guys

pause

#46.

hey is that the Hornets?

they all look off

#11.

again?

#2.

I guess so

pause

#00.

I would love to win right now
I would really really love to win

they stare at the Hornets

#46.

anyone wanna pass?

#2.

…sure

they get a ball and pass in silence for a little bit

#8.

    (singing to Schoolhouse Rock*)*
    WE THE PEOPLE
    IN ORDER TO FORM A MORE PERFECT UNION

#8 & #00.

    ESTABLISH JUSTICE
    ENSURE DOMESTIC TRANQUILITY

#8, #00 & #2.

    PROVIDE FOR THE COMMON DEFENSE
    PROMOTE THE GENERAL WELFARE AND
    SECURE THE BLESSINGS OF LIBERTY

#8, #00, #2 & #11.

    TO OURSELVES AND OUR POSTERITY
    TO ORDAIN AND ESTABLISH
    THIS CONSTITUTION
    FOR THE
    UNITED STATES OF
    AMERICA

#8.   **#00.**

    that was fun!   talk about a deep cut

#46.

    what was that

#11.

    um the preamble

#00.

    we had to memorize it

#2.

    in 5th grade

#11.

    and like perform it one by one in front of the whole school

#8.

    in assembly

#00.

    it was my nightmare

#2.

    it was my Nam

#8.

    people say that all the time but I don't get it

#2.

---

* A license to produce THE WOLVES does not include a performance license for SCHOOLHOUSE ROCK's version of THE PREAMBLE. The publisher and author suggest that the licensee contact ASCAP or BMI to ascertain the music publisher and contact such music publisher to license or acquire permission for performance of the song. If a license or permission is unattainable for SCHOOLHOUSE ROCK's version of THE PREAMBLE the licensee may not use the song in THE WOLVES but may create an original meoldy for the lyrics. For further information, please see Music Use Note on page 2.

it's something my grandpa says about my grandma's cooking

#8.

like nom?
like nom nom nom?

#2.

no I think like um

#00.

Vietnam
they're talking about Vietnam
like something's really hard it's like Vietnam

> #25 *walks on*
> *she has a buzzcut*

#25.

hey!

	#11.			#2.		

#8.   #11.   #2.
                 whoa!   #00.   wow!   #46.
OMIGOSH   oh my god   oooh

#25.

sorry I didn't think we were playing

#11.   #00.

holy shit!   you look so great

#25.

what

#2.

your hair

#25.

oh
yeah
how long have you guys been here?

#46.

don't worry about it

#8.

what did you do to your hair??

#25.

oh I
buzzed it
sorry
I thought we were going to have to forfeit so I

#46.

I think we're good
right
we have 6

#25.

    yeah

    wow

    I guess so

    ...Coach here?

#11.

    haven't seen him

#25.

    oh right

    it's his weekend on base

#8.

    wow he gave us that schedule so long ago

#25.

    ok

    ...

    ok

    I'll go talk to the ref

    ...

    I guess we're playing

    I guess we're on

            #25 *jogs off*

#11.

    man I can't believe we're actually gonna play

#2.

    yeah

    I can't tell if I want to or not

            #8 *gets a text*

#00.

    I'm so ready you guys

    I've like never felt this ready

#8.

    NO!!

            #8 *bursts into tears*

            they all stare at her

#2.

    (going to comfort her)

    hey

    shhh

#8.

    (through sobs)

    Tulsa

#2.

    it's ok

    it's ok

#8.

    (through sobs)

    Tulsa

    it's in Tulsa

#2.

    God only gives us what we can handle

#11.

    what's in Tulsa?

#8.

    nationals

    they're in Tulsa

#46.

    what?

#00.

    that blows

#11.

    what happened to Miami?

#8.

    (nodding)

    Emma just texted me

#2.

    …that really really stinks

    but you know what?

    someday you'll get to go to Miami

        #13 *jogs in*

#13.

    helloooo good people

#11.

    look who made it

#13.

    of course I did

    of course of course

    I thought we would forfeit but nopedy nope nope

#2.

    now we have 7

#46.

    an alternate!

#13.

    (re #8)

    is she ok?

#2.

nationals are in Tulsa

#8.

(*sniffling*)
I'm never going to go to Disney World

#2.

don't say that

#13.

yeah
yeah
hahahahaha
yeah

#11.

…are you on crack or something?

#13.

um
yeah
no
totally
haha
no
I'm great
I uh
haven't been sleeping
very much but uh
coupla asthma attacks
but
yeah I'm good
all good

      #25 *runs back on*

#25.

ok guys it's cool we're on

#13.

dude!! your hair!!

#25.

oh
yeah

#13.

dude!

#2.

why'd you do it??

#25.

oh I uh guess I wanted a change
it's so easy in the morning

#11.

I bet

#13.

whoa

#8.

did like a barber do it?

#25.

no
I actually
I did it myself

#13.

whoa whoa whoa

#25.

(to #8)
are you ok?

#8.

nationals are in Tulsa

#25.

really?

#13.   **#2.**

wait you gave yourself a buzzcut??   wow

#8.

like Mulan

#25.

(nods)
haha yeah
with my dad's razor

#13.

Coach Frank's razor rides again!

#11.

you did that all by yourself?

#25.

yeah
yeah
well I guess
I guess like Louise helped

#13.

...Louise?

#25.

yeah
she uh
she's shaved her head before so I thought she'd
and she like got the back of my neck

#25.

my uh she called them my
(blushing)
my blind-spots

#2.

...can I feel it?

#25.

uh
sure

       #2 *feels it*

#2.

it's soft
it's so soft

#13.

let me see

       #8 *feels*

#8.

omigosh it's like a baby duck it's so soft

       #11 *feels*

#11.

that feels so cool

       #13 *feels*

#13.

wow
totally like a baby duck

       #00 *feels*

#00.

you look really awesome

#25.

thanks
it's so easy I just like shower and that's it
no ponytail
no hair icicles

#2.

maybe I'll shave my head

#25.

yeah!
yeah
...well you guys wanna warm-up?

#11.

yeah   **#13.**

                        yeah   **#8.**

                                          yeah

they get in a circle and begin their warm-up
total silence for a while
it feels really good to do the warm-up again

#11.

(looking off)
guys is that Coach Patrick?

#8.

omigosh
it's Coach Patrick

#13.

whoa there are a lotta people over there all of a sudden

#25.

oh
yeah
my dad like texted all the other parents
on their little group text

#2.

I thought he gave a really beautiful speech

#11.

Coach Patrick?
yeah

> **#8** *waves*

#8.

guys
guys he's waving

> *they all wave and shout hi/hello/etc*

#13.

oh wowww who's that weirdo witch lady sitting next to him

#46.

that's um that's my mom

#13.

oh
...right on right on

#00.

cool cape

#46.

yeah
she's never come to a game before
I'm sorta nervous

> **#46** *waves at her*

#2.

hey isn't that Louise?

#25.

    (blushing)
    yeah!
    she came for like
    moral support

#11.

    cool

#25.

    yeah
    ...she like
    she's lost like a lot of
    like her older brother
    she um found him in their garage
    so uh
    she's been pretty cool
    actually
    she's been pretty cool

        pause

#13.

    I've never like
    I've never had anyone

#11.

    like not even a grandparent?

#13.

    no
    well I guess
    like some beta fish but
    I mean I know people but I've never gone to a funeral you know?
    or hadn't
    I guess

#00.

    my grandma died a few years ago
    my dad's mom

#25.

    I don't have any grandparents

#11.

    me neither

#46.

    I just have my one grandma but I don't know my dad so maybe I have 2

        pause

#2.

    my neighbor died a few years ago
    he was really nice
    he used to let me and my brothers and sisters come over and feed the birds

some of them look at #8 expectantly

#8.

> *(chipper)*
> hey! there's Kevin!

#13.

> *(thrilled)*
> dude! what a doofus!

#11.

> hey Ari and Lily are here too

#8.

> yeah
> I texted like everyone I know

#2.

> cool

> *pause*

#25.

> she shouldn't have worn headphones

#00.

> he should have like
> he should have defrosted you know

#2.

> guys

#13.

> she shouldn't have gone for a run at 6 a.m.
> with snow on the ground
> what sorta what sorta NUTjob does that

> *#7 hobbles on the field*

#7.

> sup bitches

> *slight pause*

#8.

> hey Alex

#2.

> hi

#11.

> hey

#00.

> hey girl

#7.

> *(to #25)*
> your hair!

> *#25 smiles and nods*

#13.

how you doing?

#7.

you know
ok

> *pause*

#7.

fucking weird to be here

#8.

yeah

#13.

yeah

> *pause*

#7.

(trying hard)
you guys have a huge fucking crowd!

#11.

yeah

#8.

haha

#7.

it's huge!

#25.

did you see Coach Patrick?

#7.

yeah
yeah

> *pause*

#7.

keep stretching!
I just wanted to you know
say hey

> *awkward silence*

#46.

are you ok?

#7.

yeah
I'm uh
yeah
you know

> *pause*

#7.

(brightly)
Dan's here

#2.

yeah?

#7.

uh huh
he took some time off school

#25.

where is he?

#7.

he's parking

#2.

that's great
that's so great

#7.

yeah

    awkward pause

#25.

so uh
did you hear
nationals are in Tulsa?

#7.

really?
(laughing)
that blows

    they all laugh with her

#7.

guess it's good there's no chance in hell I'll make it this year

#13.

haha yeah

    SOCCER MOM *walks on the field*
    she is manic with grief

SOCCER MOM.

hi!
hi gals!

    a small collective hi

wow
you look so
wow!
my god!
it's you guys!

it's our gals!
you're not getting any younger
you know?
you all look so
and it's just
it is so good to see you
just
like
like
like so good

       a pause
       she lets out a sharp laugh

I said
ha
listen to me
ha
"like"
ha
"like" "like" "like"
in our house we have a quarter jar
Alex I know you've seen it
a quarter for every "like"
and for "um" every "um"
and the oh the what do you
the going up? at the end? of the sentence?
what is that
but
they hate it
the girls
they just hate it
and I've tried to explain
if you're saying something is "like" something
then it isn't the same
it's just "like" it
and if you say that
and you hem and you haw and you um and you make everything?
a question?
then no matter how you know awesome
how brilliant your thought is
no one will ever take you seriously
because you sound like an idiot
and one time I said
I was mad
I was really
she didn't do the dishes or was texting at dinner or uh
(trying to remember) I don't uh

I don't
funny

     she is lost in thought
     then sudden and snapping
"MEGAN you say "LIKE" because you don't know ANYTHING about ANYTHING"
I said
"ANYTHING about ANY"
I was
I was really
and uh
Megan said to me
"like you do??"
"like YOU DO??"
and I
do I?
do I know anything about?

     she smiles and looks at the girls from very far away
     sudden to **#2**
honey
are you eating?
are you eating honey?
you've gotten so skinny
I didn't even recognize
just as long as you're eating
ok?
ok
…ok

     she gets a little self-conscious
now we want to see a win out there!
today!
win! win! win!
lots of fans
Big Fans
longtime fans came out just to see you!
how cool is that?
right?
so cool
Frank texted me and I was like
"I am In"
so none of that
none of that stuff with the Fusion
let's see some uh some smart soccer today
smart passing smart listening smart eyes
I've seen so many games
you have no idea

so many Saturdays and tournaments and practices and
And Megan's watching
Megan is

       sudden and distraught
oh
oh no I
I for
oh shoot I
I forgot to
shoot
from the trunk
the trunk!
oh god
I'm sorry
I'm so sorry
I'm
I'm so so
it's not
ok ok I'll be back in a jiff
I just forgot to
ok
I'm sorry
ok
it's ok
it's ok

      SOCCER MOM *hurries off*
      a long, long silence
      whistle

#25.

    (very small)
ok
let's uh
…
uh
me and #2 on defense to start
you're goalie
#46 striker
and uh
#11 and #13 on mid

    whistle

#7.

good luck guys

    #7 *starts to leave*

#25.

wanna do the cheer?

> **#7** *hobbles over as they huddle up*
> *silence*
> *it starts as a whisper*
> *and grows louder and louder*
> *until it feels rabid and raw and Bacchic*

#11, #25, #13, #46, #2, #7, #8 & #00.

we
are
the wolves
we are the wolves

we
are
the wolves
we are the wolves

we
are
the wolves
we are the wolves

we
are
the WOLVES
we are THE WOLVES

WE
ARE
THE WOLVES
WE ARE THE WOLVES

WE
ARE
THE WOLVES
WE ARE THE WOLVES

WE
ARE
THE WOLVES
WE ARE THE WOLVES

WE
ARE
THE WOLVES
WE ARE THE WOLVES

WE
ARE
THE WOLVES
WE ARE THE WOLVES

SOCCER MOM *walks on*
she holds a Ziploc of orange slices
they howl
they stop
they pant
they see her
or they don't

End of Play